Dress Me!

Written and illustrated
by Sarah Frances Hardy

Sky Pony Press
New York

To Sallie

Sky Pony Press books may be purchased in bulk at special discounts for sales promotion, corporate gifts, fund-raising, or educational purposes. Special editions can also be created to specifications. For details, contact the Special Sales Department, Sky Pony Press, 307 West 36th Street, 11th Floor, New York, NY 10018 or info@skyhorsepublishing.com.

Sky Pony® is a registered trademark of Skyhorse Publishing, Inc.®, a Delaware corporation.

Visit our website at www.skyponypress.com.

10 9 8 7 6 5 4 3 2 1

Manufactured in China, December 2014
This product conforms to CPSIA 2008

Library of Congress Cataloging-in-Publication Data

Hardy, Sarah Frances, author, illustrator.
Dress me! / Sarah Frances Hardy.
pages cm
Summary: As a young girl tries out a variety of career choices, from dancer to superhero, in different costumes and hairstyles, she discovers that sometimes it is best just to be herself.
ISBN 978-1-63220-423-3 (hardback) – ISBN 978-1-63220-832-3 (Ebook)
[1. Occupations–Fiction. 2. Imagination–Fiction. 3. Costume–Fiction.]
PZ7.H221447Dre 2015
[E]–dc23
2014033699

Cover design by Danielle Ceccolini
Cover illustration credit Sarah Frances Hardy

Dress me!

Tutu me.

Dancer me.

Artist me.

Monster me.

Scary me.

Superhero me.

Doctor me.

Mustache me.

Builder me.

Plumber me.

Lawyer me.

Waitress me.

Teacher me.

Diva me.

So NOT me!

Braid me.

T-shirt me.

Jeans me.

Sneakers me.

Jacket me.

Just me!